Little David's Adventure

Little David's Adventure
by
Squire D. Rushnell

Edited by
Barbara Shook Hazen

Illustrated by
Janet Stevens

WORD
EDUCATIONAL PRODUCTS DIVISION
WACO, TEXAS 76796

SQUIRE D. RUSHNELL, Vice President of Long-Range Planning and Children's Television for ABC Entertainment, is a highly regarded leader in the positive evolution of children's television. He is responsible for ABC's "After School Specials," "Weekend Specials," "School House Rock," and "Kids Are People, Too," which cumulatively have won over fifty Emmy awards.

JANET STEVENS is a children's book illustrator and long-time animal lover who has illustrated over fifteen children's books, including *The Princess and the Pea* and *Animal Fair*. Her adaptation of *The Tortoise and the Hare* was featured in 1985 on PBS's "Reading Rainbow."

BARBARA SHOOK HAZEN has written over fifty children's books, including *Even If I Did Something Awful* which received the 1983 Christopher Award for Excellence. She has worked as a children's book editor and as a consultant to "Sesame Street." Her book *Tight Times* was the premiere selection featured on PBS's "Reading Rainbow."

The names, descriptions, and any representations of the characters in this book are the protected property of American Broadcasting Companies, Inc.

Little David's Adventure
Copyright © 1986 by American Broadcasting Companies, Inc.

Library of Congress Cataloging-in-Publication Data

Rushnell, Squire D., 1938-
      Little David's Adventure.

      (Kingdom chums' greatest stories of all)
      Summary: Three friends travel back in time through their home computer to a Biblical land populated by talking animals, where they witness the shepherd David's battle against the giant Goliath.
      1. David, King of Israel—Juvenile fiction. 2. Goliath (Biblical giant)—Juvenile fiction. [1. David, King of Israel—Fiction. 2. Goliath (Biblical giant)—Fiction. 3. Animals—Fiction. 4. Space and time—Fiction] I. Hazen, Barbara Shook. II. Stevens, Janet, ill. III. Title. IV. Series.
PZ7 .R8982Li 1986   [Fic]   86-5609

ISBN 0-8499-8228-6
Printed in the United States of America.

To Marge Lane who inspired this book,
and to my inspirational shepherd Elaine Alestra.
Principally, to my supportive family
who lovingly embraced this mission:
Jinny, my wife, and Robin, Hilary, and Grant.

Chapter One

"Who can tell me what a hibernating bear has in common with a dog who buries his bone?" Mr. Jodphur paced back and forth in front of the science class. His eyes smiled as if it were a trick question.

Peter's hand shot up. Science was his best class, and this was an easy question. But Mr. Jodphur knew that, so he ignored Peter's eagerness and asked somebody else.

"Sauli, what do you think?" The whole class became as quiet as a tank of fish, waiting for his answer.

Sauli cringed. He took a wild stab. "Uh . . . because bears chew bones before they hibernate?" Sauli then tried a half-hearted laugh. Two girls giggled. Mr. Jodphur went on to his next victim as if he hadn't even heard Sauli.

Swack! Osborn Palmer smacked Sauli so hard on the back, his yarmulke was knocked sideways on his head.

"Hey, frisbee-head," Osborn hissed in a hoarse whisper, just loud enough for his hangers-on to hear, "you get the prize for the world's dumbest answer."

Osborn snickered. Sauli slid further into his seat.

Peter James, still waving his hand, glanced quickly at Sauli. He was Sauli's best friend. Poor Sauli, he was a good kid. He just didn't have any confidence in himself. Especially in dealing with big bullies like Osborn Palmer.

Most of the kids at All-Nations School, which Peter and Sauli attended, were nice. They were children of diplomats from all over the world and had good manners. But Osborn Palmer, whom Sauli had the bad luck to sit in front of, was the exception.

Peter and Sauli Ben-Shalom were both ten going on eleven and shared an interest in computers. Their parents were also friends. Peter's dad was an American diplomat to the Mideast. Sauli's father was a diplomat from Israel.

They, like the other students at All-Nations School, looked just like any other kids. They all wore blue jeans and sneakers. The same things made them laugh, and they all had similar problems. What made them different were their names. Names like Inga, Atsuko, Pierre, and Aboo. Names that reflected their different nationalities. But otherwise, All-Nations School kids were just kids.

"Okay, Peter," Mr. Jodphur finally sighed.

Peter was confident. "Bears hibernate and dogs bury bones instinctively."

"Ah, true. And what is instinct?" Mr. Jodphur's enthusiasm had dwindled, but he was still trying to keep up the dramatics.

"It means something animals know because they are born knowing it," Peter said matter-of-factly. Peter wasn't a show-off. He wasn't brainy-looking either. He just happened to be good at this kind of subject.

Just then the final bell rang. Peter jumped up and went over to his friend. "Hey, Sauli," he asked enthusiastically, "did your mother say you could come over?"

"Till 6:30," said Sauli, his eyes darting around, hoping not to see Osborn. "But not a minute later. I have to be home for supper."

"Hey, great," said Peter. "We can play around with my computer. I've got some fantastic new discs. But first we've got to pick up Mary Ann."

Mary Ann, Peter's six-year-old sister, was waiting outside the school, cradling an open shoe box in one arm and a stuffed lion in the other.

"Guess what?" she said, bubbling with excitement.

"What?" asked Peter and Sauli at the same time, as they walked toward the bus stop.

"Birdie was the best show-and-tell of all. And when Madam

Chalopin asked if he could talk, he said, 'cheep.'"

Peter smiled as he looked down at the frail little bird Mary Ann had rescued from a busy New York City sidewalk.

Peter's little sister loved animals. Real ones and unreal ones. At home she had three whole shelves filled with very special stuffed animals their father had brought back from diplomatic trips to the Mideast. To Mary Ann they were just as alive as Birdie.

"So Birdie can talk, but how high can he fly?" said Peter, winking at Sauli.

"Christopher says," Mary Ann answered, looking down at her stuffed lion, "that pretty soon Birdie will fly . . . about ten cubits."

Peter shook his head. Leaning toward Sauli, he confided, "Mary Ann says her stuffed animals tell her these weirdo words." Sauli giggled.

"What do ya know . . . it's ol' frisbee-head!" a voice suddenly taunted from behind. Osborn Palmer turned the corner, roughly grabbed Sauli's yarmulke, and began playing keep-away with it with one of his goon friends.

"Come on," murmured Sauli.

"Hey, pick on somebody your own size," protested Peter.

"Like who? You, computer-face?" sneered Osborn, tossing Sauli's head covering to another bully.

Sauli jumped awkwardly trying to grab his yarmulke. But he was off balance.

Before Sauli knew what hit him, he stumbled backwards into Mary Ann. The shoe box with Birdie in it fell to the sidewalk.

"Oh, no!" gasped Sauli.

"Poor Birdie," said Mary Ann very softly.

Gently she put the motionless little bird back in his shoe box bed. She looked as if she might cry. But she didn't.

"Good goin', klutz," Osborn sneered at Sauli. "You went and crushed her bird."

"Knock it off, Palmer," said Peter.

Osborn shrugged, then backed off. Scowling at Sauli, he said, "It's

10

your fault."

Sauli looked as if he were going to throw up.

After Osborn and his gang left, Peter turned to Mary Ann, putting his arm around her. "I don't think there's any way Birdie can live now," he said quietly.

"There is *so!*" replied Mary Ann firmly, blinking back a tear. "Birdie'll be okay. I *know* it. Besides, Christopher and Magical Mose will know what to do."

Peter nodded. He didn't want to argue, but he couldn't agree. His interest in science led him to only believe in what he could see, and what he saw was not good. Nor could he see how Mary Ann's conversations with her stuffed animals, Christopher, Magical Mose, and the others, could help Birdie.

Nobody talked on the bus. Mary Ann was humming to Birdie, while absent-mindedly arranging bits of straw from the shoe box into a pattern. Christopher sat motionless, staring at his scarlet sandals. Sauli was thinking maybe Osborn was right. Maybe he was a klutz and a coward. And maybe it was his fault for not standing up to Osborn. Peter, looking out the bus window, was deep in thought about what his father had said just that morning about the importance of settling things without fighting.

But then Peter's attention shifted to something that caught his eye, an unusual star formation in the sky. Some of the stars seemed to twinkle with colors—red, purple, orange, yellow, and pink. It was strange, because it was too early for stars.

When they got to Peter and Mary Ann's apartment, the children headed for the playroom where they spent most of their time after school.

They patted Luke, the family basset hound, who usually lay in the middle of the floor between Peter's and Mary Ann's sides of the room.

Peter's computer and the shelves with all his science book collections were on one side. Mary Ann's shelves, filled with stuffed animals, were on the side with the window seat.

Mary Ann began tending to Birdie. She talked softly to him about everything being all right, as she surrounded him with her favorite stuffed animals—Christopher, her loving lion with the glistening blue eyes; Magical Mose, her snappy-looking tiger with his purple and white checkered bow tie and wing-tipped shoes; and Little David, her cute raccoon with sneakers and an orange and white checkered headband. It was almost as if Mary Ann believed her stuffed-animal friends could help Birdie.

"Don't worry. You'll get better," she said.

Peter and Sauli watched as Mary Ann stroked the limp little bird's head.

"Osborn's right. It's all my fault," said Sauli, thinking sadly about what had happened that afternoon.

"It's *not* your fault, Sauli. It's Osborn's," said Peter to his friend.

"Yeah, but I should have stood up to him," Sauli replied.

Looking at her stuffed lion, Mary Ann said, "Birdie will get better, won't he, Christopher?"

Peter looked sympathetically from his sister to Sauli, then to Mary Ann again. He shook his head.

"Mary Ann," Peter started to explain, "it doesn't look like Birdie's breathing. And if an animal doesn't breathe . . . well, it's scientifically impossible for it to be alive."

"Christopher and Magical Mose said he'll be okay, and I believe them," she replied firmly. At that moment, something from the window caught Peter's eye.

"Hey, Sauli, c'mere," shouted Peter, motioning his friend to come to the window. "Look at those different colored stars . . . I saw them when we were on the bus."

"Gee, maybe it's the Big Dipper," said Sauli.

"Naw, can't be," said Peter. "The Big Dipper is in the northern sky."

"Hey, let's look at your astronomy disc," said Sauli.

"Good idea." Peter jumped up and reached for the computer disc. "Here, you set it up. I'll mark down the stars."

Pad and pencil in hand, Peter got on his knees on the window seat and excitedly marked little crosses on the paper.

Doot, doot, doot. Peter now at the computer typed small x's onto the screen, trying to recreate the star formation.

Mary Ann was doing that funny thing again. She was absent-mindedly arranging bits of packing straw from Birdie's box into a strange pattern. It was the same pattern she made with everything lately, from the peas on her plate to the pebbles in the schoolyard.

Peter went back to the window to check the star formation again. As he returned, he thought he noticed a similarity between Mary Ann's pattern and the strange star pattern.

Peter shrugged, looked sympathetically at his sister, then at the digital clock: 5:58 exactly. Doot, doot, doot. He frantically typed x's still trying to duplicate the star formation.

Time after time, Peter tried a slightly different pattern. Each time the computer screen read "Try again."

"Come on, give up," said Sauli.

"Just one more," Peter kept telling Sauli, who was beginning to fidget.

"It's almost 6:15," said Sauli. "I've got to get home soon."

Then something even stranger happened. The computer started to whir all by itself, just as Mary Ann, shoe box in hand, looked out the playroom window, her face glowing mysteriously.

Peter jumped up. "Something funny's going on," he said, shaking his head at Sauli.

"You better believe it." Sauli shook his head and looked at Mary Ann.

She walked as if in a trance. First she placed the shoe box with Birdie in it on the floor next to Luke, the dog. Then she went to Peter's bookshelves and pulled down a large, dusty book that had always been in the family. Laying the book on the table in front of the computer, she moved the cursor key as if she knew exactly what she was doing.

"Com'on, Mary Ann. Don't touch the computer when I

15

have . . . ," said Peter, his eyes widening, ". . . a program
. . . in."

"It's a word!" exclaimed Sauli.

Peter sat back amazed. With each keystroke, the light that came
from the stars outside the window grew brighter and more colorful.
The breeze from the open window quickened and gusted until it
became a strong wind.

Doot, doot, doot. Mary Ann's pigtails swayed with the wind. Her
eyes were locked on the computer screen as she moved the cursor to
make a line to connect the x's.

It was like a connect-the-dot picture that looked like this:

```
X         X   X   X XXXX
X       X X   X X   X
X     X   X   X X   XXX
X       X X     XX   X
XXXX    X       X    XXXX
```

Now the mysterious light from the stars focused into a bright
beam, made of all the colors in the rainbow, and came right inside
the window. It fell first on the big book and stayed there for a
moment.

Then the light beam fell on Christopher, Mary Ann's kingly
stuffed lion, who began to fade in its glare. Then he disappeared
completely!

Luke, lying on the floor, seemed to perk up.

Peter rubbed his eyes. They had to be playing tricks on him. Then
he mouthed the letters on the screen, "L . . . O . . . V . . . E."
They *were* the same as Mary Ann's strange patterns!

Another incredible thing—the computer was working all by itself.
This was not scientifically possible, thought Peter!

Doot, doot, doot. The image of Christopher was now appearing
on the computer screen.

Peter *really* couldn't believe his eyes. He gaped at the screen, then at Mary Ann, who giggled, "Hi, Christopher," as if nothing extraordinary were going on.

"Sauli, what's happening?" said Peter nervously.

Sauli gulped, too astounded to speak.

Little David and Magical Mose, Mary Ann's stuffed raccoon and tiger, one at a time were caught in the beam of brightly colored light. They too disappeared, only to reappear on the computer screen.

Desperately, Sauli looked at the clock as if it held an answer to the weird things that were going on. It was 6:27.

"I've really got to go home now," insisted Sauli.

But before Sauli could get on his way, Peter gasped, "Look!"

The blinding beam of light was engulfing Mary Ann. Now she too was fading.

"Mary Ann!" Peter yelled above the wind just as she disappeared completely. "Mary Ann?" Peter said almost inaudibly as she reappeared, pig-tailed and smiling, on the computer screen.

"Mary Ahhhhhh!" Peter could no longer hear the sound of his own voice. The wind was drowning it out. His eyes were closed tight, stung by the strong wind and blinded by the shining light. The last thing Peter heard was Sauli saying, "It's 6:27 . . . g-g-got to go." But Sauli didn't move toward the door because he also was fast disappearing.

"This can't be happening," said Peter. "But it is." He was looking himself up and down and realizing that he was on the other side of the computer screen, looking out.

"I c-c-can't stay," Sauli whimpered.

His voice was drowned out by a mellow, stronger one greeting them. "Hello, Peter. Hello, Mary Ann. Hello there, Sauli."

"A . . . a . . . a . . . lion just said h-h-hello to me," stammered Sauli.

"Not an ordinary lion," said Mary Ann in her usual bubbly way. "It's Christopher." Unlike her brother and Sauli, Mary Ann didn't seem a bit amazed at what was going on.

"Your stuffed animal? Oh, yeah, I recognize the sandals," said

Peter, trying to make a joke of it. Christopher was also now wearing a long scarlet robe adorned with a heart of red and white checks.

Magical Mose, Mary Ann's tiger, was dressed differently too. In addition to his usual bow tie and wing-tipped shoes, he now wore a purple cape and carried a checkered wand.

Magical Mose spoke in a friendly, enthusiastic voice. "Hahaa! Look how your faces shine with light, as Moses' face did when he came down from the mountaintop to speak with the children of Israel a long time ago."

"How do *you* know about Moses," asked Peter, then catching himself, ". . . ah, Magical Mose?"

"Instinct," replied Magical Mose with a sort of knowing grin.

"Remember, Peter?" added Christopher. "Instinct is something animals know about because they're born knowing it."

Peter thought it strange that Christopher was repeating back to him something he himself had said earlier in science class.

"We animals," continued Magical Mose, "have the inborn knowledge of our ancestors who witnessed The *Grrrreatest* Stories of All. Knowledge that comes alive in this magical place." As he swept his wand upward, the breeze rustled in the trees like music.

Peter looked around. He wondered where they were. They seemed to be in a clearing in a lush tropical garden, thick with green leafy plants and bright flowers. Flowers Peter had never seen before. The clearing was like the hub of a wheel. From it, seven paths spun off in different directions.

"Where in the world are we?!" exploded Peter, unable to contain his curiosity.

Christopher gazed at Peter with large, glistening eyes. "This is a place where time has no boundaries," the lion said in a soothing voice. "Where flowers bloom in winter and animals can talk." With that Christopher winked at Mary Ann.

"They're the Kingdom Chums," said Mary Ann proudly.

"Yes, the Kingdom Chums," smiled Christopher. "Very special animals who have been sent here to take you back into The Greatest

Stories of All, stories our forefathers saw with their own eyes and have passed on to us."

"In this magical place, history comes alive," continued Magical Mose. "You can step into a story that happened long, long ago." Then with a flourish of his wand, he added, "A place where journeys are not merely across miles but across imagination."

The tiger and the lion paused to look at the children's faces.

"Peter, Mary Ann, and Sauli, you have been chosen to ride the Kingdom Chums' Love Light to relive one of The Greatest Stories of All," said Christopher.

"Oh boy! Like in a play! Where are we going?" asked Mary Ann excitedly.

"The only place I want to go is home!" said Sauli nervously.

"Wait, Sauli," cried Mary Ann. "How can we turn down a chance like this?"

"And a little child shall lead them," Christopher murmured to Magical Mose. The lion and tiger smiled knowingly at each other.

"I still don't get it," said Peter, shaking his head. "What does that have to do with us?"

"You shall see," said Christopher in a voice firm, yet loving. He motioned to Little David who was aways off down one of the paths. "Little David will take you on your first journey and return with you."

"Do you have a phone here?" asked Sauli, now wide-eyed.

"Hiyo, Sauli. It's time to be jolly," Little David said. Mary Ann's raccoon stepped forward wearing a pair of orange overalls in addition to his headband and sneakers.

"Little David, I knew we'd find you here," shouted Mary Ann cheerfully.

Little David's voice was that of a strong, confident kid about ten or eleven. "The magic and meaning of your very first trip," said Little David, speaking in rhyme as he put his paw on Sauli's shoulder, "will sort out your feelings and foster friendship." Little David then did a shuffle with his feet like a boxer and motioned for the children to follow him to the start of one of the paths. "All aboard the Kingdom Chums' Love Light," shouted Little David with his paw cupped to the side of his mouth. "Com'on, Peter."

For a second, Peter hesitated. Who ever heard of going on the other side of a computer screen, let alone going on a journey with a bunch of talking animals? It didn't make sense.

But he was curious. Besides, he thought, in this dream, or whatever it was, what choice did he have?

"Hurry, Peter," said Christopher. "Little David is the Kingdom Chum of courage. You wouldn't want to miss his story."

Magical Mose gave Peter a light nudge. "We'll see you later. And remember," he shouted after him, "you mustn't become separated from Little David. He's your guide into . . . and out of your journey."

"Bye, Christopher. Bye, Magical Mose," shouted Mary Ann.

Christopher raised his paw skyward, and suddenly the wind and light grew in intensity. Little David and the children were once again engulfed in the whirling wind and multi-colored beam of brilliant light that pulled them down the garden path.

The wind whipped at the children's hair. The bright light made them squeeze their eyes shut. There was a feeling of fantastically fast movement.

"We must be going a trillion miles an hour," gasped Sauli.

"Naw," said Peter sensibly. "Nothing can go faster than the speed of light. Somebody said if anything passed the speed of light, 186,000 miles a second, it would go right past time."

"Wh-wh-where are we going, Little David?" asked Sauli nervously.

"Oh, about three thousand years ago," replied Little David calmly.

Peter blinked.

Meanwhile, back in the playroom, the computer whirred and the title of the big old book was reflected on the computer screen. It was *The Greatest Stories of All.*

The wind and the rainbow-colored light beam came through the

window and hit the book. The cover flipped open. Pages flashed by, stopping at "The Story of Little David's Adventure."

Luke, the children's dog, lifted an ear as if listening for someone, something. The shoe box with Birdie in it lay next to him. The digital clock still read 6:27.

Chapter Two

The wind and bright light faded. It got very dark. Mary Ann, Peter, and Sauli were surrounded by shadowy black silhouettes. Nothing could be seen except the merest suggestion of light in the distance.

"What I'm standing on feels like grass!" whispered Sauli. He squeezed Peter's hand, which he had unthinkingly grasped as they traveled inside the light beam.

"And what I'm smelling smells like sheep," said Mary Ann, who was holding Peter's other hand.

Just then a lamb bleated, confirming what Mary Ann suspected. And a bird chirped. It was sunrise, the dawn of a new day, in a pasture in a time long ago.

"I wonder where Little David is," said Peter, looking around, his eyes adjusting to the increasing daylight.

"Come on . . . this way," said Mary Ann, sniffing something else and tugging at her brother. "I'm hungry."

Mary Ann and Peter found Little David behind a big rock, cooking over a campfire.

"Good morning," he said, smiling at the amazed looks on their faces. "You're just in time."

"Wh-wh-where are we, Little David?" asked Sauli nervously.

"Not far from Bethlehem," he replied.

"Bethlehem?" asked an astonished Peter. "Bethlehem, Israel?"

"Yes," replied Little David. "That's where I live."

"I come from Israel too," said Sauli proudly.

"I have seven brothers," Little David went on. "I'm the youngest, so I get the job of tending the sheep."

"How old are you?" asked Peter.

"Same as you," said Little David.

Peter thought Little David seemed pretty mature for an eleven-year-old. He acted more like a senior in high school.

"Don't you get scared being out here alone?" asked Sauli.

"Nah," said Little David lightheartedly. "Nothing out here in nowheres . . . 'cept sheep and hungry ol' bears."

Sauli shivered.

To change the mood, Little David smiled and said, "How about some music? Mary Ann, hand me that harp, will you?"

Little David began strumming soothing melodies on his hand-made harp. He accompanied himself, singing the verses of some of his own psalms, or songs.

Peter was impressed with Little David's talents and became lost in the words of his songs.

"Thou art my strength," went one verse. "I sing praises unto Thee. You are my defense, a God of mercy unto me."

CRACK!

There was the sudden sound of tree limbs cracking!

Sauli jumped. Peter sat bolt upright. Mary Ann moved closer to Peter.

Quick as a flash, Little David was on his feet. In one graceful move, he dropped his harp and picked up a club.

He motioned the children to stay where they were while he waited, every muscle alert.

CRACK!

The unknown creature continued to move through the brush. Its heavy, growl-like breaths grew louder and scarier as it came closer.

Then the creature burst through the branch barrier. It was a huge brown bear, tantalized by the smell of food cooking. The bear's yellow fangs were bared. Spittle dropped from his large mouth.

The bear eyed Little David and then the children and growled

deeply.

"Ahhhhhnnn," whined Sauli.

Peter's chest was so tight he could hardly breathe.

The huge bear paused. He looked at the sheep, then back at Little David and the children, who stood like statues made of stone.

Then, as if testing his new opponents, the bear stepped slowly towards them on all four legs.

"Grrrowl!"

"Help, he's going to eat us!" Sauli yelled as he bolted in the opposite direction.

The bear followed Sauli with his eyes and rose on his hind legs.

"Grrrowl!"

In that instant, Little David did a quick shuffle with his feet and leapt toward the huge bear who was more than three times his size! "Yaaahhh!"

Little David jumped upwards and forward as quick as lightning. He swung his club downward, striking the snarling bear on the head.

THUD!

The bear faltered, more startled than hurt. Then the bear shuffled off, probably deciding to look elsewhere for breakfast.

"Yea, yea!" yelled Peter, slapping Little David on the back.

"You sure showed him, Little David," shouted Mary Ann.

Sauli, about ten feet away, jumped up and down. He was happy, yet ashamed of himself for having run away.

Little David looked over at Sauli knowingly. Then he said, "Thanks, Sauli!"

"Huh?" said Sauli, looking at Little David with questioning eyes.

"Thanks for getting the bear's attention and distracting him for me," said Little David, putting his paw on Sauli's shoulder.

Sauli smiled weakly. "That's okay."

"Boy, he sure was huge!" said Peter.

"Yes, he was," agreed Little David. "I'd say about six cubits tall.."

"Cubits?" said Peter, furrowing his brow and looking at Mary

Ann. Cubit was one of her favorite weird words.

"Cubits," repeated Mary Ann, matter-of-factly.

"What's that?" asked Sauli.

"A cubit is, oh, about this long," demonstrated Little David, pointing from his elbow to the tip of his paw. "That's how we measure things here."

"A six-cubit bear?" said Peter, still trying to figure it all out. "So many strange things are happening. It's like a dream or something."

"That b-b-b-bear wasn't a dream," said Sauli. "He was going to eat us. Wasn't he going to eat us, Little David?"

"I don't believe so," said Little David confidently, then lapsing into rhyme. "Bully beasts of nature, roaring down on thee, are more the frightened creature . . . ," Little David shuffled his feet, ". . . when courage is what they see."

Little David put both paws against Sauli's shoulders and added, "Once they find out that their growl doesn't scare you because you have faith in the power within you, the beasts themselves usually back off."

Sauli nodded as if he understood. But he didn't really.

Just then a voice from the distance called, "Halloo!"

"Somebody's coming," said Mary Ann excitedly.

"It's two guys—I mean, two foxes," observed Peter.

"Halloo, Little David," hollered one of the foxes breathlessly.

"We've been sent by your father," said the other as they approached. "He wants you to come home right away."

"What's the matter?" asked Little David anxiously. "Is everything all right?"

"Oh, there's nothing wrong," the first fox reassured him, as they walked up to him. "It's just that Samuel, the prophet, is at your house and he wants to see you."

"As you wish," replied Little David. He motioned for the children to help him gather his things together.

"You better hurry and see what Samuel wants," urged the second fox nervously. "I'll stay and tend your sheep."

"Come on." Little David motioned to Peter, Mary Ann, and Sauli, as they headed toward Bethlehem with the first fox.

"What's a prophet, Little David?" asked Mary Ann as they walked along.

"A very wise man, Mary Ann," he replied.

"Samuel *knows,*" added the fox respectfully, rolling his eyes upwards, pointing to the sky.

"You see, Samuel is the wisest prophet in our country," explained Little David. "He told our King Saul that he was going to be king several years before it happened."

"You mean, he can see into the future, like ESP?" asked Peter.

"I guess you could say that," said Little David.

"Saul? You have a king named Saul?" asked Sauli, astounded.

"Yes, Sauli," smiled Little David. "Almost the same as you." Sauli looked proud. He grinned at the thought that he had almost the same name as a king.

"Tell me what you know about Samuel's visit to Bethlehem," Little David then asked the fox.

"He arrived late yesterday," said the fox eagerly. "As word spread, all the villagers came out to see him. Some trembled at the sight of him."

"What does he look like?" asked Mary Ann.

"Well," said the fox, "he has very white feathers and big eyes that can see right into you."

"Sounds like an owl," observed Peter.

"He asked to see Jesse, your father," the fox continued. "I crowded up to the window of your house and could hear everything."

Peter tried to picture in his mind what the fox described.

"Sitting at the head of your long table, Samuel asked that your brothers be brought to him," the fox went on. "One by one, he asked them questions, you know, as if he were looking for something."

"He sounds mysterious," said Sauli.

The fox nodded, "When Eliab was brought before Samuel . . ."

"Eliab is my oldest brother," Little David interrupted to explain.

". . . it was as if someone were inside Samuel, speaking through his mouth. He looked right at Eliab, with those big eyes, and his voice was deep as he said, 'I have refused him.'"

"Uh-oh, I bet Eliab wasn't too happy about that," said Little David.

"You're right. Eliab looked mighty angry," said the fox messenger. "Especially when Samuel told your brother, 'Some look at outward appearances, but the Lord looks at the heart,' and then waved Eliab away."

"What about my other brothers?" Little David asked.

"All rejected. Then Samuel asked to see you, the youngest."

"I wonder what he wants," said Peter.

Little David shook his head slowly and said, "I don't know."

"Well, *I* think it's something *very* important," said Mary Ann.

"Ha ha, maybe he has ESP about *your* future, Little David," wisecracked Peter.

No one laughed. Everyone looked at Peter silently as if, by accident, he had just come up with the reason for Samuel's visit.

Chapter Three

"Boy, am I thirsty," said Sauli, who was the first to spot the well as they came down a dusty road to the center of Bethlehem.

Little David led them to the water and showed them how to scoop it up with a dipper-shaped gourd.

"Hey, Sauli, it's not exactly the *big* dipper," joked Peter, holding up the gourd. He flicked some water on Sauli, who flinched, then giggled.

"I'm hungry," said Mary Ann.

"Our house is just a little way down the street," said Little David, pointing and leading the way. "We'll get you something to eat."

"Do you think S-S-S-Samuel likes people?" Sauli whispered to

Peter.

"Listen, Sauli, I still haven't figured out what we're doing here," Peter whispered back, looking disbelievingly at the villagers.

Peter thought it was similar, but different, to the time his parents took Mary Ann and him to a recreated seventeenth-century town at Plymouth Rock, Massachusetts. There all the people were dressed up as Pilgrims. Here all the townfolk were animals dressed as people were three thousand years ago.

As they walked down the narrow cobblestone street, donkey-drawn wagons passed them, and villagers paused to look at Little David. It was as if they all felt something important was going to happen. Two lady geese, wearing shawls over their heads and robes, eyed Little David and gabbled softly as they passed.

"Look, a lot of people, I mean animals, are gathered at that house," said Sauli, pointing to a clay-colored stone building.

"That's my house," said Little David.

"The villagers have gathered to see why Samuel has called for Little David," said the fox, his voice quivering.

As Little David walked toward them, the crowd parted to let him and the children through.

Inside the house, his brothers, all raccoons, looked at Little David solemnly. His father nodded a silent greeting. At the head of the heavy plank table sat a wise-looking, white-feathered owl. Peter quietly gasped, "He *is* an owl."

"Come in, Little David. Sit down. We've been waiting for you," said the owl in a voice full of authority. His big eyes were riveted to Little David's as he motioned for Little David to sit next to him.

"These are my friends, Peter, Mary Ann, and Sauli," said Little David. The owl Samuel nodded.

For several long minutes, Samuel just sat quietly, staring into Little David's eyes. It was as if he were waiting for something.

Little David's father and brothers looked on expectantly.

Mary Ann noticed it first and drew in a breath. Then the others saw it. It was a golden glowing light that seemed to shine all around

Little David. It was as if the sun shining through the window had struck him with a spotlight.

Then, in a deep voice, as though someone were speaking through him, Samuel nodded toward Little David and said, "This is he. The spirit of the Lord comes upon you, from this day forward."

Samuel lifted a small pitcher and anointed Little David by sprinkling a few drops of oil on his head.

Peter, standing next to Little David, looked around the room. Little David's father was proud. His brothers appeared a bit awed, but pleased. All except Eliab. Eliab looked angry, Peter observed.

Then Samuel rose slowly from his chair. Without a single word, he left the house. Some of the townfolk who had been waiting outside followed him.

Everyone in Little David's family looked awkwardly at each other, not knowing quite what to say.

Little David spoke first. "Well, what do you think, Mary Ann?"

"I'm still hungry!" said Mary Ann, rubbing her stomach.

Everyone laughed. Everyone but Eliab.

Peter noticed that the sun was beginning to set in Bethlehem. He turned to his friend and asked, "Hey, Sauli, what time is it?"

Sauli looked down at his watch. "It's 6:27." Then he looked back up at Peter with a puzzled expression. That was the exact time it had been when they started on their journey. Sauli then shook his watch and listened to it to see if it was still running.

Meanwhile back at Peter and Mary Ann's apartment, their dog Luke lay on the playroom floor in front of the computer, next to Birdie in the shoe box.

Luke's ears perked up. The sound of wind once again rustled through the room. The beam of rainbow-colored light from the star formation outside the window once again moved across the room.

Luke whimpered slightly and wagged his tail.

The beam of light fell on the open book and the wind flipped several pages.

The digital clock read 6:27 P.M. Still.

33

Chapter Four

To Peter, it seemed as if he had looked into the sun and was momentarily blinded by the light.

He looked around. He was walking on a dusty road.

Mary Ann was riding on a donkey led by Little David.

Sauli was still shaking his watch and looking bewildered.

"Maybe it's 6:27 in the *morning,*" said Sauli, noting that it was now daytime. But he didn't look convinced.

"Whew, this sure is weird," said Peter.

"This isn't weird, it's fun!" squealed Mary Ann, holding the reins of her donkey like a real cowgirl.

Peter and Sauli ran up to Little David. "Where are we going?" asked Peter.

"We're off to see my brothers at the battlefront," he said, "to bring them . . ."

"Battlefront?" Sauli cut in.

"What happened to your house . . . in Bethlehem?" Peter asked at the same time.

"Whoa, wait a minute!" said Little David. "We stayed in Bethlehem for several months."

"We did?" exclaimed Peter. "You mean we just skipped past and don't remember several months?"

"We stayed there until King Saul had to go to war against the Philistines," Little David continued.

"To w-w-w-war?" said Sauli nervously.

". . . and my father has now asked me to take food supplies to my brothers at the battlefront," Little David finished.

"My mom would be really mad if I went to war without asking," groaned Sauli, nervously looking at his watch.

"Come on, you guys, cheer up," shouted Mary Ann. "We're going to have a picnic on the way."

"Peter, guess what?" said Sauli anxiously.

"Don't tell me," groaned Peter. "It's 6:27."

"Yup."

"Boy, I bet Einstein never thought of *this* theory," Peter muttered. "Exceed the speed of light and Sauli's watch stops." Then he added, "How can we zoom back three thousand years and then several months ahead? It doesn't make sense!"

"Do you have any peanut butter and jelly sandwiches for our picnic, Little David?" asked Mary Ann.

"What funny things you eat," he laughed.

"I see it! I see it!" said Mary Ann excitedly, her thoughts turning from food to the scene in front of her.

In the distance, as far as the eye could see, was an encampment with rows and rows of tents. There was the woody smell of campfires and there was a low din of noise.

It certainly *looks* real, thought Peter to himself.

"They don't look like they're fighting," said Sauli to Little David. He sounded relieved.

"I've heard they've been at a standoff for several weeks," said Little David as they approached the camp.

Suddenly a fox soldier halted them, jabbing a pointed spear. "Who goes there!"

Sauli thought the spear and the question were directed at him. "Sauli Ben-Shalom. All-Nations School. Sixth grade."

As the puzzled guard wondered whether to let them pass, Little David asked where he might locate his brothers and was directed down a long row of tents.

The activity seemed to be picking up as they came closer to the part of the camp facing the enemy.

"Look! There's your brother Eliab," said Peter.

But before they reached Little David's brother, soldiers with alarmed looks on their faces began scurrying in many directions.

"He's coming again!" shouted one.

"Who? Who's coming again?" Little David asked the frightened fox.

"When will someone get it over with?" exclaimed another fox

soldier.

"What's going on?" demanded Little David.

"The Philistine giant!" cried another wide-eyed fox rushing by.

Looking out from the camp, Peter could see a valley between them and the tents of the Philistine army on the opposite hilltop. But he couldn't see a giant.

In the distance, he could hear a spooky, clanking sound. It was like the sound of Frankenstein's monster walking in an old movie.

CLANK, CLANK, CLANK.

A hush came over the Israelite encampment. It was so still the wind could be heard rustling through the scrub bushes. Then the clanking steps stopped, causing everyone to listen even more intently.

"What are you doing here?" demanded a gruff voice behind the children. Peter, Mary Ann, and Sauli were startled.

"Eliab, how are you?" said Little David, calmly turning to greet his brother.

"I asked, what are you doing here?" repeated the older raccoon.

"Father sent me. He wants to know how *you're* doing," replied Little David.

"You should be tending your sheep," said Eliab sarcastically. Then, scowling toward Peter, Mary Ann, and Sauli, he demanded, "Who are these creatures? Philistine spies?"

"They are friends of mine," replied Little David calmly.

Peter didn't like the gruff sound of Eliab's voice, but there was another sound at the moment drawing everyone's attention toward the enemy camp.

CLANK, CLANK, CLANK. The spooky clanking sound began again.

"Come, you cowards!" The Philistine giant then bellowed. The sound made the soldiers quiver and Sauli's eyes bulge.

Mary Ann nestled closer to her brother, who squinted into the distance.

"I hear him, but I can't see him," said Peter.

"There must be *one* among you who is not afraid!" the giant again bellowed. "If so, send him to meet me in battle. If he wins, the Philistines will be your slaves. If I win, you will surrender to us."

Then he laughed a gruesome laugh.

Little David turned to the soldiers and asked, "Who is that?"

"Goliath of Gath," said one.

"He's been making the same challenge for forty days," said another.

The first soldier added, "Instead of our two armies fighting, Goliath demands that we send just one soldier to fight him."

"He's the Philistines' most wicked warrior," said another.

"And we have sent no one to meet him?" asked Little David, amazed.

The soldiers stood awkwardly silent. Eliab looked impatient with his younger brother.

Little David asked again, "Are you telling me we have sent no one to meet this Goliath who double dares the army of the Lord?"

One soldier fox spoke up. "King Saul has offered lots of money to anyone who'll face Goliath."

Sauli perked up at the mention of King Saul, whose name was almost the same as his.

"I don't believe it!" exclaimed Little David. "We don't have a single soldier brave enough to face him?"

At that, Little David's older brother Eliab could no longer keep back his deep resentment. "Who do you think you are?" he lashed out at Little David. "And what are you doing here anyway?" He pointed his paw accusingly. "You don't belong here among soldiers."

"Father sent me with supplies for you and our brothers," said Little David quietly.

"I know you," said Eliab. "You're just a brat who came here hoping to see the mightiest soldiers in battle."

"No," said Little David. Then, after a pause, he added in a strong, confident voice, in rhyme, "But I do see your mighty soldiers rattled, fearing a giant from Gath, so I will face in battle . . . the one you call Goliath."

As Little David's words hung in the air, he gave a confident shuffle of his feet.

The crowd of soldiers buzzed among themselves:

"We have a volunteer!"

"Finally, someone will meet Goliath!"

"How can he possibly win?"

"We'll be Philistine slaves!"

"Anything is better than forty more days of this!"

Eliab curled his lip and glared at Little David. "Now you've done it, you little showoff. We'll send your broken bones back to Father."

Eliab turned to the children and added, "And those of your spy friends," before he stalked away.

Sauli watched Eliab push through the crowd and saw him stop to speak with two mean-looking guard moles. Eliab then pointed back at the children.

"Come with us to the king," a fox guard whispered to Little David, as the crowd continued to babble. "He'll want to speak with you."

As Little David, Peter, Mary Ann, and Sauli were led deeper into the camp toward King Saul's headquarters, the bellow of Goliath could still be heard reverberating, "Is there no one among you yellow-bellied cowards who will meet me?"

"Uh-oh, I think Little David's in big trouble now," Peter whispered to Sauli.

"H-h-h-he's not the only one," replied Sauli, glancing back to see Eliab glowering at him.

"Never fear," said Mary Ann cheerfully. "Little David's going to be our hero." With a carefree look on her face, she scrambled ahead to take the raccoon's paw in her hand.

Peter decided someone had to be the voice of reason. He caught up with Little David and cautioned, "Don't you think you're biting off more than you can chew, Little David?"

He smiled, "The Lord is my Shepherd, Peter."

A puzzled look came over Peter's face as he tried to figure out what Little David meant. "Look, Little David, I know you're brave," Peter went on, "but this is crazy. Don't you see? There's no way you can win against a giant."

Little David continued to smile at Peter.

"Look! You've got to face reality," pleaded Peter. "Just think, your whole country is at stake . . ."

Little David still smiled.

"Don't worry, Peter," interrupted Mary Ann. "Everything is going to be *just fine!*"

Peter shook his head in utter disbelief. How could it be "just fine"?

Chapter Five

They came to a tent much larger than the others in the camp. It was nobly striped in gold, burgundy, and white, and smelled of incense.

Mary Ann spotted a bowl of fruit and asked, "Little David, when can we get something to eat?"

He patted Mary Ann comfortingly with his paw and said, "As soon as we see the king, okay?"

Little David and the children were directed to a small room inside the big tent. On a couch lay King Saul, a stately cat. He had a pained look on his face.

"The king suffers from dreadful headaches," whispered the guard fox to the children, as if to explain the cat's grouchy look.

"Yes . . . who is it?" demanded King Saul.

"The young brave one," answered the fox, nodding toward Little David. "And his friends," he added as the king eyed Sauli, Mary Ann, and Peter closely.

Peter wondered if he was supposed to bow or something.

Mary Ann didn't bother to wonder. She went right ahead.

"How do you do, Your Majesty," said Mary Ann cheerfully as she curtsied.

King Saul stared at her with a sour look on his face.

Peter and Sauli stood like stone statues. No way will I bow now, thought Peter.

"So," demanded King Saul with a furrowed brow, "who is the warrior who has volunteered to battle the mighty Goliath to the death?"

He looked right at Sauli.

"Not me!" exclaimed Sauli, jumping backwards.

"I have, sir," said Little David firmly.

"Come here. Closer," commanded the king.

Peter, Mary Ann, and Sauli inched along behind Little David as he stepped forward.

"What?" questioned Saul. "You are but a youngster."

King Saul's words became loud and angry as he continued. "Goliath is the Philistines' most feared warrior. He's been a soldier since his youth!"

"My King, as your servant, I will fight the Philistine," Little David replied in a strong voice.

"You cannot fight this monster who has threatened us for forty days."

"That's what I told him," whispered Peter to Sauli.

"As I tended my father's sheep in the wilderness, Your Majesty, beasts attacked our flock several times. Once a bear had a little lamb in his jaws. I jumped him and fought him to the end," said Little David confidently.

"No," said Saul, "you are too young. Thinking you can go against Goliath is foolhardy."

"I have fought bears while tending my sheep," Little David continued, "and, as your servant, I will put away this heathen Philistine who has defied the armies of the living Lord!"

The king looked stunned. How could so small and youthful a volunteer come forward? And with such brave words from his lips.

"Little David can do it, sir," said Mary Ann. The king's eyes shifted. He was even more disbelieving now that the young rac-

coon's bravado was being confirmed by a little girl.

For several moments King Saul was silent. Sauli nervously shuffled from one foot to the other. Peter could hear the cat's raspy breathing.

Then King Saul raised his paw to his head, as if to change the subject, and said, "Aughh . . . these headaches . . . they're painful."

Mary Ann stepped forward. "I bet Little David's music would help, King, sir," she said, curtsying once more.

"What?" replied the king, as he watched Little David pull his instrument from a leather bag. "Well, then . . . play!" he commanded.

Little David strummed his fingers across the strings of his harp. The children sat down on the floor, listening to the soft, sweet music.

After three songs, King Saul continued to look pained. "I still have my headache," he growled in a menacing tone.

Peter wondered what happened to musicians who didn't please the king. He remembered something scary in a fairy tale about a court jester who was punished for failing to make a king laugh.

"My head *still* hurts," King Saul repeated petulantly, just to be sure that his point had been made. Sauli fidgeted nervously.

"I'll try another melody, Your Majesty," said Little David calmly, beginning to play.

Halfway through the song, Peter noticed that King Saul was still looking unhappy.

What Peter saw next made his mouth fall wide open. His little sister got up and walked right over to the cranky cat.

On the way, she picked up two hollow sticks, the kind kings used to hold scrolls, and began to strike them together rhythmically. Now Little David began to play faster in keeping with Mary Ann's quickened tempo.

"I am a child of God," Little David sang.

Mary Ann kept on increasing the beat. Then she walked over to her astonished brother and handed him the sticks. She signaled for him to play and for Sauli to clap with her.

King Saul began to perk up. His tail began swishing to the beat of the music.

Now Mary Ann began to dance as well as clap.

Little David began to sway. "Through my faith in Him, I reflect what's within . . ."

The king smiled. He was now tapping his paw on the royal couch in time to the music.

"For I am a Child of God!" Little David finished with gusto.

At the end of the song, King Saul applauded, saying, "You've done it. My headache is all gone."

Then the king stood up, put his arm around Little David, and looked at him thoughtfully, "So, you believe you can fight the giant," he said.

Little David stood a little taller and nodded.

The king sighed, then said, "All right, Little David, go. And the Lord be with you."

Mary Ann was about to say what a smart decision that was, but Saul cut her off, commanding his servants, "Bring my young warrior and his friends something to eat. And bring in my armor."

As dinner was brought in, Peter kept glancing around the room. He had the feeling he was inside some weird time warp.

Finally his curiosity got the best of him. He wanted to test whether or not this was a dream.

"Excuse me, Your Majesty," said Peter courteously. "What period of time is this? B.C. or A.D.?"

The king looked at Peter blankly.

"What?" he said impatiently. "What is B.C. or A.D.?"

"Before Christ or after?" said Peter.

"Who is Christ?"

Peter was now in a conversation he wished he had never started. "Ah . . . what I mean is . . . ," said Peter, trying to muddle through, "your furniture is very old . . . and very nice."

"Ah, yes, thank you," said King Saul.

After they ate, King Saul ordered Peter and Sauli to hold up his armor so Little David could get into it. The chest armor was heavy.

"Ouch!" yelped Sauli, struggling to raise the side of the armor he had dropped on his toe.

When the heavy metal coat was finally on Little David, Mary Ann began to giggle. "You look just like me when I wear one of Dad's shirts."

Peter and Sauli couldn't help laughing too. The bottom of the chest armor came down almost to Little David's knees.

"Here, try this on," said Mary Ann cheerfully. She picked up King Saul's brass helmet, stepped on a stool, and placed the helmet upon Little David's head. It slipped down over his eyes. They all laughed again, harder this time.

"Now you look like me when a New York Giant once let me wear his helmet," Peter burst out. Then he wondered if he should explain to King Saul that a New York Giant football player was different from a Goliath-type giant. He decided to just let it pass.

Their laughter momentarily helped relieve the tension brought on by the awareness of what Little David was facing. As Peter came back to reality, he began to consider the odds against Little David being able to come out of this battle alive. The odds were not good.

His thoughts were interrupted by Little David's saying to King Saul, "I'm sorry, sir. I cannot wear your armor."

Little David then took off the helmet and metal coat, and added, "I've never been trained to fight with armor. I will face Goliath with my own weapons."

The king shook his head in utter disbelief.

Again Peter was getting that gnawing feeling at the bottom of his stomach, the feeling you have when you have to stand up in front of a big audience and make a speech, the feeling of being about to be sick.

"So," King Saul asked quietly, now respecting and accepting the young raccoon's determination, "what *will* your weapons be?"

Little David reached with his paw to the rope belt of his toga. "This!" he said, holding up his sling. It was a long leather strap with a pocket. By placing a stone in the pocket and grabbing both ends of the strap, one could sling the stone like a bullet.

Now ready to believe anything, King Saul merely nodded, thinking that despite all his good intentions the brave, misguided youngster probably had little time to live.

Little David said a quick goodbye to King Saul and left his headquarters. Outside, he began giving orders like a born leader.

"Peter, see if you can find me a strong stick from that woods over there. One a little shorter than my staff. Mary Ann, take that water bag to the creek and fill it with water."

Then he turned to Sauli and said, "Sauli, you're going to help me find the ammunition for my weapon."

Sauli looked pleased to have such an important job, but a bit unsure of what was expected of him.

At the creek's edge, Little David reached down into the cool, clear spring waters and picked up a smooth stone. "I need five stones this size," he told Sauli, holding up the one as a specimen.

Enthusiastically, Sauli stepped into the water to do as he was asked.

"Little David?" asked Sauli, after a few minutes of looking for just the right size stones.

"Yes?"

"Aren't you afraid?"

"Yes . . . but I have faith, Sauli. Faith in the power within me." Sauli thought for a second.

"The only way to overcome fear," continued Little David, "is by believing with all your might in the spirit and the strength God has given you. Have faith and your fear will diminish."

For a minute, while that was sinking in, there was only the splashing sound of the creek waters.

Then Mary Ann called from a big rock at the creek's edge, "The water bag's full."

"And I've found a perfect stone," shouted Sauli proudly. "And another."

One by one, Little David took the stones and rubbed them in the palms of his paws the way a baseball pitcher rubs a baseball. Then he put all five stones into his leather shepherd's pouch.

"How's this, Little David?" asked Peter, holding up a stick from a tree branch. "It's about one cubit long," he added, with a big grin in Mary Ann's direction.

"Good job, Peter," said Little David, noting that the stick was just right.

Sauli squinted. "Compared to Goliath it looks like a toothpick!"

Little David smiled. "Right, Sauli. It doesn't seem like much of a weapon, does it?"

"Hey," said Peter, "I bet you just want Goliath to *think* it's your weapon, huh, Little David?"

Little David smiled again. Then he did that shuffle with his feet. "Peter, my man, you're onto my plan."

Chapter Six

"We'd better go," was all Little David said.

Peter, Mary Ann, and Sauli knew that this was it, the time they'd been dreading.

"You stay here," Little David ordered as they got to the front lines of the Israelite army, the same place where earlier they had heard Goliath bellow his challenge.

The word spread like wildfire, as Little David stepped forward, ready to fulfill his destiny. Soldiers rushed to the hilltop to watch. They buzzed and whispered among themselves. If this mere youngster were to fail, as he was almost certain to do, they would all become captives of the Philistine army. So much rested on such small shoulders.

The word had already reached the Philistines, for Peter noted that the enemy encampment on the opposing hill was stirring with excitement.

"I feel kinda sick to my stomach," muttered Sauli. Then he tried to remember what Little David had said about fear and didn't feel quite so queasy as he made himself walk up to Little David and pat him on the back.

"Go get 'em," said Sauli, thinking this was probably the last time he would ever see his raccoon friend Little David . . . alive.

Mary Ann reached up, kissed Little David on his cheek, and said, "You can do it, Little David."

Peter just said, "Good luck."

Little David held the stick in his right paw and his staff in his left. The sling was in his belt. The pouch containing the stones hung across his shoulder, down his right side.

Little David turned to glance back at the Israelite army.

His brothers Abinadab and Shammah stood with Eliab. They each gave a small smile of encouragement, because they wished him well yet didn't want to invite the scorn of Eliab, who coldly stared at his youngest brother.

Now the Philistine soldiers, an army of rats, were becoming raucous in their excitement of anticipated victory. Their yells echoed and re-echoed throughout the valley.

Little David began walking slowly and deliberately to the bottom of the valley. Because of his size and modest clothing, he could hardly be seen among the bushes.

A low din of moaning and anxiety shuddered through the Israelite army as the soldiers heard in the distance the familiar sound which always preceded the coming of Goliath—CLANK, CLANK, CLANK.

Little David was already in the valley when the Philistine giant appeared on the hilltop from among the ranks of cheering rats.

The Israelite forces became quiet. You could hear the gasps as Goliath strode into view.

Peter swallowed hard. This giant must have been almost seven cubits tall. That was over nine feet! "Wow! Look at the size of him," exclaimed Peter.

The giant wart hog that strode down into the valley was indeed awesomely huge and armor-covered. With every step, the brass bottom of his chestplate clanked ominously against the metal coverings on his thick legs. CLANK, CLANK, CLANK.

Strapped to one arm of the giant was a heavy iron shield on which was painted the face of a horrible serpent. In the opposite hand, he grasped a long, dangerous-looking spear. From his metallic belt hung a deadly sword, which swung back and forth like a pendulum.

Peter wondered if his own eyes were open as wide as Sauli's. And if he looked as scared. Even Mary Ann, who was never fazed by anything, appeared apprehensive as she edged closer to Peter.

CLANK, CLANK, CLANK. Each giant step grew louder, till the sound of metal against metal echoed throughout the valley as Goliath came closer.

It was getting hot. Flies were buzzing in the air around Peter's head, making him swat irritably.

As Little David stepped slowly across the floor of the valley, the cheers of the enemy rats seemed distant. He could hear his own breathing.

The wind hissed through the bushes and caused tiny whirlwinds along the sandy ground.

The clanking resounded in Little David's ears. As he moved forward, he began to recite aloud the psalm he had written to express his confidence and faith:

"The Lord is my Shepherd, I shall not want . . ."

CLANK, CLANK, CLANK. Goliath was now at the bottom of the hill, crossing the valley toward Little David.

"He maketh me to lie down in green pastures . . . beside the still waters," Little David continued, his breathing increasing in anticipation of battle.

In the center of the valley, Little David stopped. He moved clockwise so that his back was to the sun. He stood motionless, both feet firmly planted on the ground.

CLANK, CLANK, CLANK. Goliath was now less than a hundred feet in front of him. Little David could see Goliath's mean, reddened eyes and his yellow fangs.

CLANK, CLANK, CLANK. Little David could now hear the giant wart hog's heavy breathing.

Little David stood like a stone statue. Only his lips moved slightly as he continued his psalm: "Yea though I walk through the valley of the shadow of death . . ."

CLANK, CLANK. Goliath stopped, sniffed the air, and listened the way wild animals do. Now both army camps were breathlessly quiet.

"Who is here?" roared Goliath, looking around.

". . . I will fear no evil . . . ," Little David whispered.

Then Goliath spotted Little David and moved toward him. CLANK, CLANK, CLANK.

"What? A ruddy youth?" the giant snorted. "With sticks?"

". . . for Thou art with me!" said Little David.

CLANK, CLANK. Goliath took two steps closer.

"Do you think I am a dog you can hit with a stick!" he sneered.

The giant's breathing was very heavy now. Little David stood absolutely still.

Spitting as he bellowed, Goliath shouted, "Come to me and I will give your flesh to the birds."

On the hilltop, Peter shuddered as "birds, birds, birds," echoed like thunder off the valley walls. Then he heard Little David's answer, which sounded small by comparison.

"You come at me with your spear and your sword," said Little David, "but I come at you in the name of my Lord."

Now Little David's words were ringing in unison with the echo, "I raise up my rod, but the battle is God's!"

Goliath was furious. He snarled and began to move within striking distance of his small opponent.

But Little David was quick! Just as he had been in the field with

the bear. Instantly he tossed the stick upwards with his right paw, while dropping his staff and pulling the sling from his belt.

Goliath watched the stick as it rose up, up, directly into the sun. For a moment, the powerful giant was blinded.

In that brief moment of distraction, Little David dashed forward to meet his enemy. He grasped a smooth stone in the shepherd's bag and put it into the pouch of the sling.

Peter could feel every muscle in his body tighten.

Mary Ann prayed, "Please . . ."

Sauli gritted his teeth.

In a split second, Little David was swinging the sling, hurtling the stone to its mark.

With deadly aim, the stone struck the leathery forehead of the giant, just below the rim of his helmet.

"Aaaagggghhhh!" Goliath of Gath gasped and rolled his eyes upwards. Then his knees buckled and, like a fallen tree, the Philistine warrior fell helplessly backward.

As his hulking body struck the hardened clay ground, the sound of smashing metal ricocheted off the valley walls, and clouds of dust rose.

The crowds on both sides were silent in utter astonishment.

Deftly, Little David pulled the giant's sword from its scabbard and finished the battle. And the life of the Philistine.

Chapter Seven

Both sides now responded noisily. In the Philistine camp, fear and shock caused pandemonium. The soldiers, fearful of the unseen power of the youthful warrior, ran amuck.

But from the Israelite camp came cheers! The celebrating soldiers threw their helmets into the air and danced hand-in-hand jubilantly.

Toward the front of all this commotion, Peter, Mary Ann, and Sauli were locked in a quiet embrace. No one said anything. They were too relieved, proud, and joyful to speak. Full of feeling, they only half noticed the streams of soldiers now rushing past them, scampering down to the valley to touch the young hero and carry him high above their heads and chant, "Yea, yea, yea!"

It was Peter who spotted Little David's head bobbing above the soldiers and called out, "Here they come!"

But the soldiers didn't stop, and Little David didn't seem to see them. The children were jostled by the excited mob.

"Little David! Little David! Over here!" Mary Ann yelled in vain.

As Little David's legions of noisy fans carried him off, Peter wondered how they were ever going to get back together. After all, Peter thought uneasily, Little David is our guide into and, I hope, out of this crazy time warp—or whatever it is.

At the same time, Sauli noticed something of more immediate concern. Eliab was moving threateningly toward them along with some of his meaner mole buddies.

"Quick!" Sauli shouted to Peter and Mary Ann. "Into the crowd!"

"What's the matter?" asked Peter.

Then, looking back, he saw that Eliab and two of the moles were chasing them and closing in.

"Stop! They're spies!" shouted one of the moles.

"Faster!" shouted Sauli. "They're catching up."

"Ohhhhh," screamed Mary Ann. Trying to go too fast, she tripped and fell. "Little David!" were her last words before the wind was knocked out of her.

Eliab and the moles were only a few steps away.

Then, just as Eliab reached out to grab Mary Ann, Little David, riding upon the shoulders of the crowd, turned his head in the children's direction. Mary Ann's voice must have reached him after all.

SSSShwishhh! The blinding multi-colored Love Light suddenly returned. A faint outline of the kindly lion Christopher, his paw raised upwards, seemed to appear inside the beam. There was the sound of speed. A sound like the pages of a book flipping!

For the first time since their adventures began, Peter was glad all this was happening.

As the light became brighter and the sound of the wind grew stronger, Peter pulled Mary Ann and Sauli closer to himself.

"Birds! I hear birds," said Sauli. Then the wind sounds quieted, and the light became less intense.

"Hahaa! You have just finished your first journey into The *Grrrreatest* Stories of All," said Magical Mose with a flourish of his wand that made the birds sing in unison.

"Oh, Magical Mose, it was wonderful!" said Mary Ann, grinning at the tiger with the purple cape and wing-tipped shoes.

"And as you return to this magical place, many more journeys with the Kingdom Chums await you and your friends," said Christopher.

"They do?" asked Peter. As his eyes began to clear, Peter recognized the garden with the seven paths where they had started their journey with Little David.

"Yes, they do," replied Magical Mose.

"Hey, where's Little David?" said Sauli, looking around.

"Hahaa. You'll see him again. But for now," said Magical Mose, almost singing along with the birds he had made sing, "you must go back."

"And don't forget what you've learned," reminded Christopher, placing his left paw on Sauli's shoulder while raising his right one.

Again the swishing winds and bright light of many colors engulfed the children. Sauli tried to look at his watch, but the light was too dazzling.

Chapter Eight

This time when the wind sounds stopped and the light faded, the dog Luke was licking Peter's hand. "Hey, that tickles!" said Peter.

Sauli blinked. His eyes finally focused on his watch. "Guess what?" said Sauli. "It's still 6:27!" He looked up at the digital clock

over the computer which said the same thing. Then he and Peter both said, "Wow!"

"All right, now we've got to figure out what happened," said Peter, who always liked to figure things out.

Mary Ann wasn't listening. She was staring out the window at the star formation that spelled "love," as it began to fade.

Birdie was now cheeping and hopping inside the shoe box.

"See, Peter," she said. "Birdie wants to say hello to you. He's all better."

"How can he be?" said Peter. It wasn't scientifically possible, and yet, there Birdie was, chirping and hopping and looking amazingly recovered.

Mary Ann stroked the mane of her stuffed lion. "Christopher says all things are possible with faith." She then smothered her Kingdom Chum lion with a big hug.

Sauli wasn't listening. He was still studying his watch and muttering, "I still don't believe it. Now my watch is moving again, and it's 6:28. I better get going because I promised I'd be home at 6:30."

Peter and Mary Ann walked Sauli to the door. "See you tomorrow," Peter said. Then he added, "Will you be okay getting home?"

"Sure," said Sauli confidently. "It's only three blocks."

Sauli's apartment was two blocks south and one block east. It was already getting dark.

But Sauli was feeling good as he walked home. Unlike Peter, he didn't spend much time questioning what happened, even if it was hard to believe. For sure, it was the most exciting day of his life so far.

Sauli turned the corner to his block. Suddenly he was hit hard in the chest.

A frisbee lay teetering on the sidewalk.

"Well, look who's going around knocking down frisbees," said Osborn Palmer who, along with some of his nasty buddies, was blocking the entrance to Sauli's building.

"Looks like your old friend the bird crusher," taunted one of the

buddies.

Sauli stopped still. He looked in both directions. There was no escape. Osborn took a step closer. So did his buddies.

Just one day earlier, in a similar situation, Sauli might have cried or even fainted. But not today. Today things were different.

Calmly, Sauli bent down, picked up the frisbee, and walked right up to Osborn Palmer. As he did, he said very softly to himself, "I shall fear no evil."

"Hello, Osborn. I think this is yours," said Sauli confidently. But instead of handing it to him, Sauli tossed the frisbee straight up in the air.

Osborn looked absolutely astonished. He turned his face up to watch the frisbee and found himself looking into a glaring street lamp.

Osborn Palmer stepped back involuntarily, covering his eyes from the blinding street light. But there was no sidewalk under Osborn's foot. It was too late by the time he realized he was stepping off the curb.

KERSPLASH! With arms flailing, Osborn fell clumsily into a mud puddle. Sauli smiled slightly as he walked on into his building.

The doorman, who had been watching and was obviously impressed with the *new* Sauli Ben-Shalom, saluted him.